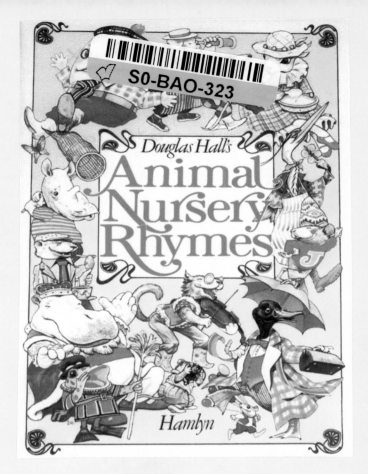

Douglas Hall's
Animal Nursery Rhymes

Hamlyn

First published 1979
Fifth impression 1985
Published by The Hamlyn Publishing Group Limited
London · New York · Sydney · Toronto
Astronaut House, Feltham, Middlesex, England

ISBN 0 600 36593 X
Printed in Czechoslovakia
52105

Douglas Hall's
Animal Nursery Rhymes

HAMLYN
London · New York · Sydney · Toronto

Hey diddle, diddle

Hey diddle, diddle,
The cat and the fiddle,
The cow jumped over the moon;
The little dog laughed
To see such sport,
And the dish ran away with the spoon.

Little Miss Muffet

Little Miss Muffet
Sat on a tuffet,
Eating her curds and whey.
There came a big spider,
Who sat down beside her,
And frightened Miss Muffet away.

Ding, dong, bell

Ding, dong, bell,
Pussy's in the well.
Who put her in?
Little Johnny Green.
Who pulled her out?
Little Tommy Stout.

What a naughty boy was that
To try to drown poor pussy cat,
Which never did him any harm,
But killed the mice in his father's barn.

I love little pussy

I love little pussy, her coat is so warm,
And if I don't hurt her, she'll do me no harm.
So I'll not pull her tail, nor drive her away,
But pussy and I very gently will play.
She shall sit by my side and I'll give her some food,
And pussy will love me because I am good.

I saw three ships

I saw three ships come sailing by,
Come sailing by, come sailing by.
I saw three ships come sailing by,
On New Year's Day in the morning.

And what do you think was in them then,
Was in them then, was in them then?
And what do you think was in them then,
On New Year's Day in the morning?

Three pretty girls were in them then,
Were in them then, were in them then.
Three pretty girls were in them then,
On New Year's Day in the morning.

And one could whistle, and one could sing,
And one could play on the violin.
Such joy there was at my wedding,
On New Year's Day in the morning.

Rub-a-dub-dub

Rub-a-dub-dub,
Three men in a tub;
And who do you think they be?
The butcher, the baker,
The candlestick-maker;
They all jumped out of a rotten potato,
'Twas enough to make a man stare.

Round the rugged rock

Round and round the rugged rock
The ragged rascal ran.
How many R's are there in that?
Now tell me if you can.

13

Wee Willie Winkie

Wee Willie Winkie runs through the town,
Upstairs and downstairs, in his nightgown;
Rapping at the window, crying through the lock,
'Are the children all in bed, for now it's eight o'clock?'

Little Poll Parrot

Little Poll Parrot
Sat in his garret,
Eating toast and tea;
A little brown mouse
Jumped into the house,
And stole it all away.

One, two, buckle my shoe

One, two,
Buckle my shoe;
Three, four,
Knock at the door;
Five, six,
Pick up sticks;
Seven, eight,
Lay them straight;
Nine, ten,
A big fat hen.

The Queen of Hearts

The Queen of Hearts,
She made some tarts,
All on a summer's day.
The Knave of Hearts,
He stole the tarts,
And took them clean away.

The King of Hearts
Called for the tarts,
And beat the Knave full sore.
The Knave of Hearts
Brought back the tarts,
And vowed he'd steal no more.

Jack and Jill

Jack and Jill went up the hill
To fetch a pail of water;
Jack fell down and broke his crown,
And Jill came tumbling after.

Then up Jack got and home did trot,
As fast as he could caper.
They put him to bed and plastered his head
With vinegar and brown paper.

Bobby Shaftoe

Bobby Shaftoe's gone to sea,
Silver buckles at his knee;
He'll come back and marry me,
Bonny Bobby Shaftoe!

Bobby Shaftoe's bright and fair,
Combing down his yellow hair;
He's my love for evermore,
Bonny Bobby Shaftoe!

Ladybird! Ladybird!

Ladybird! Ladybird! fly away home;
Your house is on fire, your children all gone;
All but one, and her name is Ann,
And she crept under the pudding pan.

Four stiff-standers

Four stiff-standers,
Four dilly-danders,
Two lookers, two crookers,
And a wig-wag.

Diddle, diddle, dumpling

Diddle, diddle, dumpling, my son John,
Went to bed with his trousers on;
One shoe off, and one shoe on;
Diddle, diddle, dumpling, my son John.

Jack Sprat

Jack Sprat could eat no fat,
His wife could eat no lean,
And between them both, you see,
They licked the platter clean.

Peter White

Peter White will never go right.
Do you know the reason why?
He follows his nose wherever he goes,
And that stands all awry.

29

To market, to market

To market, to market, to buy a fat pig,
Home again, home again, jiggety-jig;
To market, to market, to buy a fat hog,
Home again, home again, juggety-jog.

30

Peter, Peter, pumpkin-eater

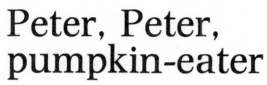

Peter, Peter, pumpkin-eater,
Had a wife and couldn't keep her.
He put her in a pumpkin shell,
And there he kept her very well.

The house that Jack built

This is the house
that Jack built.

This is the malt
That lay in the house
that Jack built.

This is the rat
That ate the malt
That lay in the house
that Jack built.

32

This is the cat
That killed the rat
That ate the malt
That lay in the house
   that Jack built.

This is the dog
That worried the cat
That killed the rat
That ate the malt
That lay in the house
   that Jack built.

33

This is the cow
    with the crumpled horn,
That tossed the dog
That worried the cat
That killed the rat
That ate the malt
That lay in the house
    that Jack built.

This is the maiden
    all forlorn,
That milked the cow
    with the crumpled horn,
That tossed the dog
That worried the cat
That killed the rat
That ate the malt
That lay in the house
    that Jack built

This is the man
   all tattered and torn,
That kissed the maiden
   all forlorn,
That milked the cow
   with the crumpled horn,
That tossed the dog
That worried the cat
That killed the rat
That ate the malt
That lay in the house
   that Jack built.

This is the priest
   all shaven and shorn,
That married the man
   all tattered and torn,
That kissed the maiden
   all forlorn,
That milked the cow
   with the crumpled horn,
That tossed the dog
That worried the cat
That killed the rat
That ate the malt
That lay in the house
   that Jack built.

This is the cock
  that crowed in the morn,
That waked the priest
  all shaven and shorn,
That married the man
  all tattered and torn,
That kissed the maiden
  all forlorn,
That milked the cow
  with the crumpled horn,
That tossed the dog
That worried the cat
That killed the rat
That ate the malt
That lay in the house
  that Jack built.

This is the farmer
   sowing the corn,
That kept the cock
   that crowed in the morn,
That waked the priest
   all shaven and shorn,
That married the man
   all tattered and torn,
That kissed the maiden
   all forlorn,
That milked the cow
   with the crumpled horn,
That tossed the dog
That worried the cat
That killed the rat
That ate the malt
That lay in the house
   that Jack built.

Solomon Grundy

Solomon Grundy,
Born on Monday,
Christened on Tuesday,
Married on Wednesday,
Took ill on Thursday,
Worse on Friday,
Died on Saturday,
Buried on Sunday.
This is the end
Of Solomon Grundy.

Pussy cat, pussy cat

Pussy cat, pussy cat, where have you been?
I've been to London to look at the queen.
Pussy cat, pussy cat, what did you there?
I frightened a little mouse under her chair.

Old King Cole

Old King Cole
Was a merry old soul,
And a merry old soul was he;
He called for his pipe,
And he called for his bowl,
And he called for his fiddlers three.

Every fiddler, he had a fiddle,
And a very fine fiddle had he;
Oh, there's none so rare
As can compare
With King Cole and his fiddlers three.

40

Mary, Mary,
quite contrary

Mary, Mary, quite contrary,
How does your garden grow?
With silver bells and cockle shells,
And pretty maids all in a row.

Humpty Dumpty

Humpty Dumpty sat on a wall,
Humpty Dumpty had a great fall.
All the king's horses and all the king's men
Couldn't put Humpty together again.

Old Mother Hubbard

Old Mother Hubbard
Went to the cupboard
To fetch her poor dog a bone;
But when she got there
The cupboard was bare,
And so the poor dog had none.

She went to the fruiterer's
To buy him some fruit;
But when she came back
He was playing the flute.

She went to the hatter's
To buy him a hat;
But when she came back
He was feeding the cat.

She went to the tailor's
To buy him a coat;
But when she came back
He was riding a goat.

The dame made a curtsy,
The dog made a bow;
The dame said, 'Your servant,'
The dog said, 'Bow-wow.'

45

One, two, three, four, five

One, two, three, four, five,
Once I caught a fish alive,
Six, seven, eight, nine, ten,
Then I let it go again.
Why did you let it go?
Because it bit my finger so.
Which finger did it bite?
The little finger on the right.

Here we go round the mulberry bush

Here we go round the mulberry bush,
The mulberry bush, the mulberry bush.
Here we go round the mulberry bush,
On a cold and frosty morning.

This is the way we wash our hands,
Wash our hands, wash our hands.
This is the way we wash our hands,
On a cold and frosty morning.

This is the way we wash our clothes,
Wash our clothes, wash our clothes.
This is the way we wash our clothes,
On a cold and frosty morning.

This is the way we go to school,
Go to school, go to school.
This is the way we go to school,
On a cold and frosty morning.

This is the way we come out of school,
Come out of school, come out of school.
This is the way we come out of school,
On a cold and frosty morning.

Girls and boys come out to play

Girls and boys, come out to play,
The moon doth shine as bright as day;
Leave your supper and leave your sleep,
And come with your playfellows into the street.
Come with a whoop, come with a call,
Come with a good will or not at all.
Up the ladder and down the wall,
A halfpenny roll will serve us all.
You find milk, and I'll find flour,
And we'll have a pudding in half an hour.

Georgie Porgie

Georgie Porgie, pudding and pie,
Kissed the girls and made them cry,
When the boys came out to play,
Georgie Porgie ran away.

Goosey, goosey gander

Goosey, goosey gander,
Whither shall I wander?
Upstairs and downstairs
And in my lady's chamber.
There I met an old man
Who would not say his prayers.
I took him by the left leg
And threw him down the stairs.

Hickory, Dickory, Dock!

Hickory, dickory, dock!
The mouse ran up the clock.
The clock struck one,
The mouse ran down,
Hickory, dickory, dock.

Rain, rain, go away

Rain, rain, go away,
Come again another day,
Little Tommy wants to play.

Doctor Foster

Doctor Foster went to Gloucester
In a shower of rain.
He stepped in a puddle, up to his middle,
And never went there again.

Muffin Man

Oh do you know the muffin man,
The muffin man, the muffin man,
Oh do you know the muffin man,
Who lives in Drury Lane?

Oh yes, I know the muffin man,
The muffin man, the muffin man,
Oh yes, I know the muffin man,
Who lives in Drury Lane.

Pat-a-cake, pat-a-cake

Pat-a-cake, pat-a-cake, baker's man,
Bake me a cake as fast as you can.
Roll it and pat it and mark it with 'B',
And put it in the oven for Baby and me.

Jerry Hall

Jerry Hall,
He was so small,
A rat could eat him,
Hat and all.

Old Mother Goose

Old Mother Goose,
When she wanted to wander,
Would ride through the air
On a very fine gander.

Little Bo-peep

Little Bo-peep has lost her sheep,
And can't tell where to find them;
Leave them alone, and they'll come home,
Bringing their tails behind them.

Little Bo-peep fell fast asleep,
And dreamt she heard them bleating;
But when she awoke, she found it a joke,
For they were still a-fleeting.

Then up she took her little crook,
Determined for to find them;
She found them indeed, but it made her heart bleed,
For they'd left their tails behind them.

It happened one day, as Bo-peep did stray
Over a meadow hard by,
That there she espied their tails, side by side,
All hung on a tree to dry.

She heaved a sigh, and gave by and by
Each careless sheep a banging;
Then she did what she could, as a shepherdess should,
To fix each one back on a lambkin.

Simple Simon

Simple Simon met a pieman,
Going to the fair,
Says Simple Simon to the pieman,
'Let me taste your ware.'

Says the pieman to Simple Simon,
'Show me first your penny.'
Says Simple Simon to the pieman,
'Indeed, I have not any.'

Oh dear, what can the matter be?

Oh dear, what can the matter be?
Oh dear, what can the matter be?
Oh dear, what can the matter be?
Johnny's so long at the fair.

He promised he'd buy me a bunch of blue ribbons,
He promised he'd buy me a bunch of blue ribbons,
He promised he'd buy me a bunch of blue ribbons,
To tie up my bonny brown hair.

A wise old owl

A wise old owl lived in an oak.
The more he saw the less he spoke.
The less he spoke the more he heard.
Why can't we all be like that wise old bird?

Ride a cock-horse

Ride a cock-horse to Banbury Cross,
To see a fine lady upon a white horse;
Rings on her fingers and bells on her toes,
She shall have music wherever she goes.

Ring-a-ring o' roses

Ring-a-ring o' roses,
A pocket full of posies,
A-tishoo! A-tishoo!
We all fall down.

Little Jack Horner

Little Jack Horner sat in the corner,
Eating a Christmas pie;
He put in his thumb, and he pulled out a plum,
And said, 'What a good boy am I!'

I had a little pony

I had a little pony,
His name was Dapple Grey.
I lent him to a lady
To ride a mile away.

She whipped him, she slashed him,
She rode him through the mire.
I would not lend my pony now
For all the lady's hire.

The grand old Duke of York

The grand old Duke of York,
He had ten thousand men,
He marched them up to the top of the hill
And he marched them down again.
And when they were up, they were up,
And when they were down, they were down,
And when they were only half-way up,
They were neither up nor down.

70

Polly, put the kettle on

Polly, put the kettle on,
Polly, put the kettle on,
Polly, put the kettle on,
We'll all have tea.

Sukey, take it off again,
Sukey, take it off again,
Sukey, take it off again,
They've all gone away.

There was a little mouse

There was a little mouse
and he lived just there.
Once he went hunting
right up there.

Baa, baa, black sheep

Baa, baa, black sheep,
Have you any wool?
Yes, sir, yes, sir,
Three bags full.
One for my master,
One for my dame,
And one for the little boy
Who lives down the lane.

There was a crooked man

There was a crooked man, and he went a crooked mile,
He found a crooked sixpence against a crooked stile;
He bought a crooked cat, which caught a crooked mouse,
And they all lived together in a little crooked house.

Three little kittens

Three little kittens,
They lost their mittens,
And they began to cry,
'Oh, mother dear,
we sadly fear
That we have lost our mittens.'

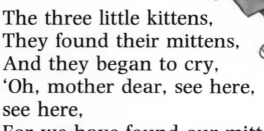

'What! Lost your mittens,
You naughty kittens!
Then you shall have no pie.
Mee-ow, mee-ow, mee-ow.
No, you shall have no pie.'

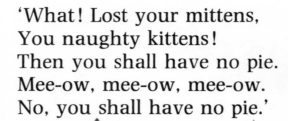

The three little kittens,
They found their mittens,
And they began to cry,
'Oh, mother dear, see here,
see here,
For we have found our mittens.'

'What! Found your mittens,
You silly kittens!
Then you shall have some pie.
Purr-r, purr-r, purr-r,
Oh, let us have some pie.'

Three little kittens,
Put on their mittens,
And soon ate up their pie;
'Oh, mother dear, we greatly fear
That we have soiled our mittens.'

'What! Soiled your mittens,
You naughty kittens.'
Then they began to sigh,
'Mee-ow, mee-ow, mee-ow.'
Then they began to sigh.

The three little kittens,
They washed their mittens,
And hung them out to dry.
'Oh, mother dear, do you not hear,
That we have washed our mittens?'

'What! Washed your mittens?
You're good little kittens.
But I smell a rat close by!
Hush! Hush! Hush!
I smell a rat close by.'

Little Boy Blue

Little Boy Blue,
Come blow your horn!
The sheep's in the meadow,
The cow's in the corn.

But where is the boy
Who looks after the sheep?
He's under a haycock,
Fast asleep!

Will you wake him?
No, not I,
For if I do,
He's sure to cry.

78

I had a little nut tree

I had a little nut tree; nothing would it bear
But a silver nutmeg and a golden pear.
The King of Spain's daughter came to visit me,
And all was because of my little nut tree.
I skipped over water, I danced over sea,
And all the birds in the air couldn't catch me.

Three young rats

Three young rats with black felt hats,
Three young ducks with new straw flats,
Three young dogs with curling tails,
Three young cats with demi-veils,
Went out to walk with two young pigs
In satin vests and sorrel wigs.
But suddenly it chanced to rain
And so they all went home again.

This little pig went to market

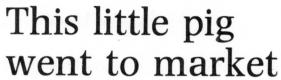

This little pig went to market,
This little pig stayed at home,
This little pig had roast beef,
This little pig had none,
And this little pig cried, 'Wee-wee-
wee-wee-wee,
I can't find my way home.'

Yankee Doodle

Yankee Doodle came to town,
Riding on a pony;
He stuck a feather in his cap
And called it macaroni.

See-saw, Margery Daw

See-saw, Margery Daw,
Johnny shall have a new master;
He shall have but a penny a day,
Because he can't work any faster.

Hickety, pickety

Hickety, pickety, my fine hen,
She lays eggs for gentlemen;
Gentlemen come every day
To see what my fine hen doth lay.
Sometimes nine and sometimes ten,
Hickety, pickety, my fine hen.

Sing a song of sixpence

Sing a song of sixpence,
A pocket full of rye;
Four and twenty blackbirds
Baked in a pie.

When the pie was opened,
The birds began to sing;
Wasn't that a dainty dish
To set before the king?

The king was in his counting-house,
Counting out his money;
The queen was in the parlour,
Eating bread and honey.

The maid was in the garden,
Hanging out the clothes
When down came a blackbird,
And pecked off her nose!
Then down came a
jenny wren
And popped it back again!

12345678910 11

Index of first lines

A wise old owl lived in an oak 64
Baa, baa, black sheep 73
Bobby Shaftoe's gone to sea 22
Diddle, diddle, dumpling, my son John 26
Ding, dong, bell 8
Doctor Foster went to Gloucester 55
Four stiff-standers 25
Georgie Porgie, pudding and pie 51
Girls and Boys, come out to play 50
Goosey, goosey gander 52
Here we go round the mulberry bush 48
Hey diddle, diddle 6
Hickety, pickety, my fine hen 88
Hickory, dickory, dock 53
Humpty Dumpty sat on a wall 43
I had a little nut tree 81
I had a little pony 68
I love little pussy 9
I saw three ships come sailing by 10
Jack and Jill went up the hill 20
Jack Sprat could eat no fat 28
Jerry Hall 58
Ladybird! Ladybird! 24
Little Bo-peep has lost her sheep 60
Little Boy Blue, come blow your horn 78
Little Jack Horner sat in the corner 67
Little Miss Muffet sat on a tuffet 7
Little Poll Parrot 16
Mary, Mary, quite contrary 42
Oh dear, what can the matter be? 63
Oh do you know the muffin man? 56
Old King Cole 40
Old Mother Goose 59
Old Mother Hubbard 44
One, two, buckle my shoe 17
One, two, three, four, five 47

Pat-a-cake, pat-a-cake, baker's man 57
Peter, Peter, pumpkin-eater 31
Peter White will never go right 29
Polly, put the kettle on 71
Pussy cat, pussy cat where have you been? 40
Rain, rain, go away 54
Ride a cock-horse to Banbury Cross 65
Ring-a-ring o' roses 66
Round and round the rugged rock 13
Rub-a-dub-dub 12
See-saw, Margery Daw 87
Simple Simon met a pieman 62
Sing a song of sixpence 90
Solomon Grundy 38
The grand old Duke of York 70
The Queen of Hearts 19
There was a crooked man 74
There was a little mouse 72
This is the house that Jack built 32
This little pig went to market 85
Three little kittens 76
Three young rats with black felt hats 82
To market, to market, to buy a fat pig 30
Wee Willie Winkie runs through the town 15
Yankee Doodle came to town 86